GOOD WORK, AMELIA BEDELIA

GOOD WORK, AMELIA BEDELIA

by **Peggy Parish**

pictures by **Lynn Sweat**

AN AVON C CAMELOT BOOK

AVON BOOKS, INC.
1350 Avenue of the Americas
New York, New York 10019

Text copyright © 1976 by Margaret Parish
Illustrations copyright © 1976 by Lynn Sweat
Published by arrangement with William Morrow and Company, Inc.
Visit our website at **www.AvonBooks.com**
Library of Congress Catalog Card Number: 75-20360
ISBN: 0-380-72831-1

First Avon Camelot Reformat Printing: September 1996
First Avon Camelot Printing: March 1980

CAMELOT TRADEMARK REG. U.S. PAT. OFF. AND IN OTHER COUNTRIES, MARCA REGISTRADA,
HECHO EN U.S.A.

Printed in the U.S.A.

OPM 10 9 8 7 6 5

For Sam and David Rogers

with love

GOOD WORK, AMELIA BEDELIA

"Amelia Bedelia," called Mr. Rogers.

"Is the coffee ready?"

"Coming right up," said Amelia Bedelia.

She poured a cup of coffee.

She took it into the dining room.

"There," said Amelia Bedelia.

"Would you like something more?"

"Yes," said Mr. Rogers.

"Toast and an egg."

"Fine," said Amelia Bedelia.

She went into the kitchen.

Very quickly

Amelia Bedelia was back.

Mr. Rogers picked up the egg.

He broke it over his toast.

"Confound it, Amelia Bedelia!"

he said. "I didn't say raw egg!"

"But you didn't say to cook it,"
said Amelia Bedelia.

Mr. Rogers threw down his napkin.

"Oh, go fly a kite," he said.

Amelia Bedelia looked surprised.

"All right," she said. "If you say so."

Soon Amelia Bedelia was out in a field.

She had a kite.

"Now that was nice of Mr. Rogers,"

she said. "I do love to fly kites.

But I better get back.

Mrs. Rogers might need me."

Sure enough, Mrs. Rogers was calling,
"Amelia Bedelia."

"Here I am," said Amelia Bedelia.

"There's a lot to do,"
said Mrs. Rogers.

"Do you know how to make bread?"

"I make good corn bread,"
said Amelia Bedelia.

"No, I want white bread,"
said Mrs. Rogers.

"You are a good cook.

Just do what the recipe says."

"All right," said Amelia Bedelia.

"Here's a list of the other things
I want you to do," said Mrs. Rogers.
"I'll be out until dinner time."
"Don't worry," said Amelia Bedelia.
"I'll get everything done."
Mrs. Rogers left.

"I'll start with that bread,"
said Amelia Bedelia.
She read the recipe.
"Do tell," she said.
"I never knew
bread did magic things."

Amelia Bedelia got everything
she needed.
Quickly she mixed the dough.

Amelia Bedelia
set the pan on the table.
"Now," she said,
"you're supposed to rise.
This I've got to see."
Amelia Bedelia sat down to watch.
But nothing happened.
"Maybe you don't like to be watched.
I'll come back," said Amelia Bedelia.

"Let's see."

Amelia Bedelia got her list.

"Clean out the ashes
in the parlor fireplace.
Fill the wood box."

Amelia Bedelia went into the parlor.

She cleaned out the ashes.

And Amelia Bedelia filled
the wood box.

"That's done," said Amelia Bedelia.

"What's next?"

She read, "Pot the window box plants.

Put the pots in the parlor."

Amelia Bedelia went outside.

She counted the plants.

Then she went into the kitchen.

"My goodness," she said.

"I need every pot for this."

So she took them all.

Amelia Bedelia potted those plants.

And she took them inside.

"Now I better tend to that bread,"
said Amelia Bedelia.

She went into the kitchen.

But the bread still sat on the table.

"Now look here," she said.

"You are supposed to rise.

Then I'm supposed to punch you down.

How can I punch if you don't rise?"

Amelia Bedelia sat down to think.

"Maybe that pan is too heavy,"
she said.

"I better help it rise."

Amelia Bedelia got some string.
She worked for a bit.
And that bread began to rise.
"That should be high enough,"
said Amelia Bedelia.
"I'll just let you stay there awhile."

Amelia Bedelia picked up her list.

"'Make a sponge cake.'"

Amelia Bedelia read that again.

"I know about a lot of cakes,"
she said.

"And I never heard tell of that.
But if she wants a sponge cake,
I'll make her a sponge cake."

Amelia Bedelia put a little of this
and some of that into a bowl.
She mixed and mixed.
"Now for that sponge," she said.
Amelia Bedelia got a sponge.
She snipped it into small pieces.
"There," she said.
"Into the cake you go."

Soon the sponge cake was baking.

"I don't think Mr. Rogers

will like this cake,"

said Amelia Bedelia.

"I'll make my kind of cake too.

He does love butterscotch icing."

So Amelia Bedelia

baked another cake.

"There now," she said.

"I'll surprise him."

Amelia Bedelia put

the butterscotch cake in the cupboard.

She put the sponge cake on a shelf.

"My, this is a busy day,"
said Amelia Bedelia.
"Let's see what's next.
'Call Alcolu. Ask him to patch
the front door screen.'"
Amelia Bedelia shook her head.
"Alcolu can't patch anything,"
she said. "I better do that myself."
She got what she needed.

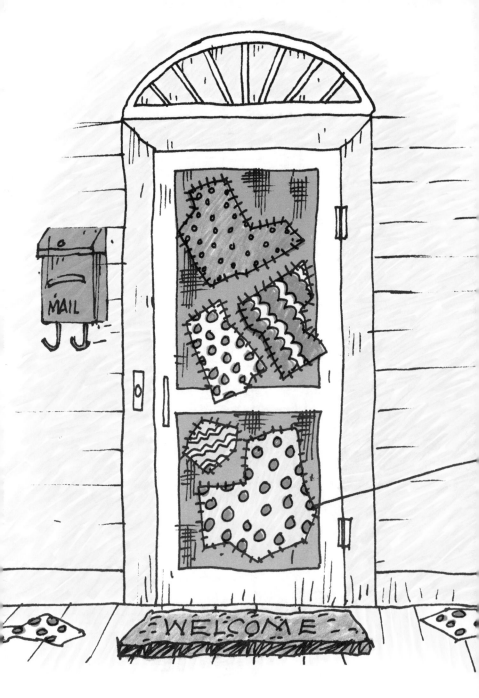

And Amelia Bedelia patched that screen.

Amelia Bedelia looked at the time.

"Oh," she said.

"I better get dinner started.

Let me see what she wants."

She read the list.

"'A chicken dinner will be fine.'"

Amelia Bedelia shook her head.

"What will she think of next?" she said.

"Well, that won't take long to fix."

Amelia Bedelia got everything ready.

She set the table.

Then she sat down to rest.

Soon Mr. and Mrs. Rogers came home.

"Amelia Bedelia," yelled Mr. Rogers.

"Coming," called Amelia Bedelia.

"What is that awful cloth
on the front door?" said Mrs. Rogers.

"You said to patch the screen,"
said Amelia Bedelia.
"Can't patch without a patch."

They went into the parlor.

"All my good pots!" said Mrs. Rogers.

"And bad ones too,"
said Amelia Bedelia.

Mr. Rogers looked at the wood box.

He shook his head.

But he didn't say a word.

They went into the kitchen.

"The sponge cake is pretty,"

said Mrs. Rogers.

"At least that's done right."

Something caught Mr. Rogers's eye.

He looked up.

"What in tarnation is that?" he said.

"The bread!" said Amelia Bedelia.

"I plumb forgot it.

Do let me punch it down quick."

She climbed up on a chair.

Amelia Bedelia began to punch.

Mr. and Mrs. Rogers just stared.

The bread plopped to the floor.

"Did I see what I thought I saw?"
said Mr. Rogers.

"You did," said Mrs. Rogers.

"Now," said Amelia Bedelia,

"dinner is ready when you are."

"Well, you can cook," said Mrs. Rogers.

"Dinner should be good."

"I hope so," said Mr. Rogers.

"I'm hungry."

"Just serve the plates,"

said Mrs. Rogers.

Mr. and Mrs Rogers sat at the table.
Amelia Bedelia brought in the plates.

Mr. and Mrs. Rogers stared at the plates.

"But, but, that's cracked corn.

It's all kinds of awful things,"

said Mrs. Rogers.

"You said chicken dinner,"

said Amelia Bedelia.

"That's what chickens eat for dinner."

Mrs. Rogers was too angry to speak.

"Take this mess away,"

said Mr. Rogers.

Mrs. Rogers said,

"Serve the cake and coffee."

Amelia Bedelia did.

Mr. Rogers took a big bite of cake.

He spluttered and spit it out.

"What in tarnation is in that?" he said.

"Sponge," said Amelia Bedelia.

"Mrs. Rogers said

to make a sponge cake."

Suddenly Mr. Rogers laughed.

He roared.

Mrs. Rogers looked at the lumpy cake.

Then she laughed too.

"But I'm still hungry,"
said Mr. Rogers.

"I can fix that," said Amelia Bedelia.

"I have a surprise for you."

"Oh no!" said Mr. Rogers.

"I can't stand another one,"
said Mrs. Rogers.

Amelia Bedelia brought in milk
and her butterscotch cake.
"Ahh," said Mr. Rogers.
"Hurry," said Mrs. Rogers.
"Give me some."
Soon the whole cake was gone.

"How do you do it, Amelia Bedelia?"
said Mr. Rogers. "One minute
we're hopping mad at you."
"And the next, we know we can't
do without you," said Mrs. Rogers.

Amelia Bedelia smiled.

"I guess I just understand your ways,"
she said.

Look for all the stories about horses . . .
by Lois Szymanski

A PERFECT PONY
78267-7/$3.99 US/$4.99 Can

At the horse auction, Niki sees a beautiful white mare that's perfect for her. But then she spots a little black horse with spindley legs and big sad eyes, and Niki must decide whether to bid for her "perfect" pony with her head . . . or her heart.

And Don't Miss

A PONY PROMISE
78266-9/$3.99 US/ $4.99 Can

LITTLE ICICLE
77567-0/$3.99 US/$4.99 Can

A NEW KIND OF MAGIC
77349-X/$3.99 US/$5.50 Can

PATCHES
76841-0/$3.99 US/$5.50 Can

LITTLE BLUE EYES
78487-4/$3.99 US/$4.99 Can

"A story snakes through this book, the violent story of how things are made—sugar, love, lonely people. Likewise, Martin Pousson's poems seem burned into being, like the tattoos that mark them, the flour for making *roux*, the scars of youth. These fire-wrought poems crackle with sex and longing, leaving a taste on the tongue, ash on the heart."
—**Priscilla Becker**,
         author of *Internal West*

"Martin Pousson's careful use of forms—from couplets to triplets to prose poems—tautens his deeply felt meditations on home and family, exclusion and loss, wounding and survival."
—**John Biguenet**,
         author of *The Torturer's Apprentice* and *Oyster*

"Here is the poet Louisiana has always wanted. Gulf Coast heat turns into huge trees and lush flora, which then turn into sex and dramatic dialogue. Desire so metamorphic inevitably slides toward hallucination. To convey experience at the edge, Martin Pousson has invented a new poetics that takes from the earlier art only its intense imagery and verbal economy. The few dozen pages of *Sugar* bring a tragic and sensuous bayou mindscape unforgettably to life."
—**Alfred Corn**,
         author of *Stake* and *Contradictions*

"With *Sugar*, Martin Pousson returns to the territory that activated his novel, *No Place, Louisiana*, recharging that fertile ground with a shift from prose to poetry. The result is a series of compressed observations, by turns satiric and heartbreaking, languorous, outraged, and tender."
—**Dave King**,
         author of *The Ha-Ha*

"The poems in Martin Pousson's debut volume of verse, *Sugar*, are achingly bittersweet, unfolding in touching fits and starts, and full of startlingly timed shocks. It's evocative of Elizabeth Bishop's *Geography III*, but with balls and more politically intrepid."
—**Richard Rambuss**,
author of *Closet Devotions*

"Martin Pousson's dirty south, chock full of fresh wounds and age-old alienation, is a pure pleasure to read again and again. For those willing to ride shotgun, just know that his road is torn to shreds. And his sugar ain't sweet. It's scorched."
—**Jake Shears**,
Scissor Sisters

"Pousson's *Sugar* shoves the edge of the sword into the bone. With poems like 'Directions' and the bare-faced grit of Louisiana's 'Live Oak,' he delves into the beginnings, the bloodline, and thrusts us forward into the ferocity of AIDS, the scars it leaves behind, the memory where 'I could kiss him anywhere / he said / except his mouth.'"
—**Olympia Vernon**,
author of *Eden* and *Logic*

"In *Sugar* Pousson has masterfully mined the infinitely complex overlapping edges of language, perception, desire, and recollection that comprise what we call experience. These are the poems of someone who has not just survived, but someone who feels impelled to thrive."
—**Thomas Woolley**,
author of *Toilet*

for my
Sister 1994
with MadLove

SUGAR

MARTIN POUSSON

suspect thoughts press
www.suspectthoughtspress.com

12/05

Copyright © 2005 by Martin Pousson

Author photograph by:
Richard Read

Cover illustration, photography, and design by:
Shane Luitjens/Torquere Creative

Book design by:
Greg Wharton/Suspect Thoughts Press

First Edition: November 2005
10 9 8 7 6 5 4 3 2 1

Library of Congress Cataloging-in-Publication Data

Pousson, Martin.
  Sugar / by Martin Pousson.
    p. cm.
  ISBN-13: 978-0-9763411-5-4 (pbk.)
  ISBN-10: 0-9763411-5-8 (pbk.)
  I. Title.

PS3616.O87S84 2005
813'.6--dc22

                                                  2005027367

Suspect Thoughts Press
2215-R Market Street, #544, San Francisco, CA 94114-1612
www.suspectthoughtspress.com

Suspect Thoughts Press is a terrible infant hell-bent to burn the envelope by publishing dangerous books by contemporary authors and poets exploring provocative social, political, queer, spiritual, and sexual themes.

ACKNOWLEDGMENTS

MAD MOJOS: Georges Borchardt, Greg Wharton, and, especially, Ian Philips

ILLUMINATORS: Ryan Brock, Terry Clewley, Michael Cunningham, Christopher DeKuiper, Scott Fontenot, Eric Gabriel, Larry Glade, Lis Harris, Richard Howard, David Johnson, Anthony Lioi, Lesley McHardy, Richard Read, Tom Woolley, and, especially, Jason Sellards

DARKO BOYS: Andy Bailey, Joe Marci, Eric Polito, and the Hoodoo Guru, Stephen Kijak

Grateful acknowledgment is also made to the following publications in which some of these poems first appeared in different forms: *Cocktail*, *Epoch*, *Icon*, *ReVisions*, *The Louisiana Review*, *New Delta Review*, *Parnassus*, and *Transfer*.

For my mother
— the Immaculate Heart —

For my father
— the Sacred Heart —

For my sister
— the Rock-n-Roll Heart —

And for the City of New Orleans
— the Eternal Heart —

CONTENTS

SUGAR

Where I come from, they smash cane
to make sugar, burn flour to make *roux,*
burn crosses to make a point.

Something sick in me wants to go back,
to lay out in the Louisiana sun,
to eat *boudin* with my fingers,

suck out of a crawfish head,
hear some Creole boy pull
on my name like taffy.

But there's a payback for going home:
my hair will kink,
and my skin turn red

then Mama will call me "Sugar,"
look though me like I was a glass
of warm beer. No, people down there

don't see any use for a boy who's queer:
you can't smash him,
can't burn him to make something else.

EVANGELINE

We have a lot of myths here in Louisiana:
about the tongues of the Mississippi

snapping up all the Indians
who danced on the Delta long before us;

about Iberville and Bienville naming
each found village like Adam naming the animals;

about the chicken-foot scratches
on the tomb of the Voodoo Queen;

about the spontaneous combustion of Jazz
in the 1890s, about holes in the Kingfish's

socks and in the shining blue pasties
of his brother's whore, the state's official

First Stripper; and about the Sunshine Bridge,
hunching its back on the way

to nowhere—spanning no river, nearing
no *ville*, serving no purpose. Then comes

Evangeline, the myth with a moral,
sitting under a live oak for decades

snaking through her like silt
through a bayou. Waiting so long

and watching for the irises of the man
she had memorized, she *became* a live oak,

ruler of centuries. Cut through her,
they say, and you see rings. But let her rot

and you see a scarlet azalea and a mockingbird
with eyes like mirrors.

HERS

Tired of his radio station,
weekly allowances and pointless jokes, tired

of escorted routine trips even
to the supermarket, the laundromat and the mall,

of frequent checkup calls
to make sure she stayed home while he worked,

tired of the brisk, brutal, unannounced visits
to her side of the bed,

she staged a coup and conceived with intent
a revenge baby, all hers.

In the white-tiled hospital room,
Mama repeated her manifesto:

her child, *hers*. Dared
her husband to name me "The Third" after his father

and him. Denied a dynasty, designed my name
by herself, even refused

to feed me from breasts he touched.
She fed me formula milk, clothed me

in cotton gowns with stitched-on wings.
A doll, I was a tiny doll

an alien baby, but hers, her own sweet
emancipation baby,

a pocket angel sent to lift her
out of her husband's reach,

her private baby Jesus,
her little hero who'd deliver her

from her man,
deliver her from herself.

THE COVENANT

She's kissed the tomb of Marie Laveau,
swapped her soul for black thread
she wields like an anaconda
sewing his lips shut

Man said enough.
Time she do the talking.

A G E 5, N. A V E. L

This is all I remember:
peanut butter and banana sandwiches,
the rag I would soak in the tub

then suck the water out of,
onions I hated to see in my food,
Mama's Heavenly Hash, frozen Kool-Aid on a stick.

Also, our next-door neighbor's
hairless groin — white as marshmallow.
He was twelve when he put on his father's

chrome sunglasses, lay back in the velour
La-Z-Boy. "Come to Daddy," he said,
"Put your mouth here."

TABOO

Don't talk about how much your father makes.
Don't tell anyone about the oil well on the farm.
Don't walk barefoot outside.
Don't go in the bathroom with your sister.

Don't tell anyone your uncle is in jail.
Don't tell anyone your aunt is really a blonde.
Don't touch yourself there.
Don't touch yourself there with your sister in the house.

Don't eat chocolate.
Don't drink strawberry soda.
Don't go in Daddy's dresser.
Don't mess with Mama's makeup kit.

Don't ask your grandma for money, and when she
        gives it to you,
Don't mention it to your cousins.
Don't go to the neighbors so much—they'll think we
Don't want you here.

EULOGY I

I see him near a bayou, teaching me to kiss dogs,
to speak Cajun, chop okra
to be suspicious of furniture and strangers.

I see his feet, the ones I loved to scratch,
gone plastic with calluses.
They carried him over rice fields and gravel roads,

carry him now to me. I put my lips
against his feet, rub my face against his toes.
He swears he can't feel a thing.

"If you're looking for heaven,"
he once told me,
"You won't find it no place."

Marble-eyed, eternal old man,
he could tell you a lot.
But he never could have known

his namesake would husband nothing,
father nothing, marry and divorce
ideas, drop his grin, his accent,

drop no more than a love note
in his grandfather's copper casket
and laugh the laugh of an old man.

SLEEPWALKER

I bumped into a wall, dropped
an egg on the kitchen floor. What a

mess. Doesn't she do enough cleaning?
I woke with her with running water,

sucking on a face cloth in the tub
at 3 a.m. Sweet Jesus, she's fixing

to beat some manners into me. She spills
rice grains on the linoleum, puts me down

kneeling. She doesn't see the film
over my eyes. I'll go on sleeping

until the seeds prick the skin of my knees
like tiny vertebrae. When I wake

I'll think I'm kneeling on my own
brittle spine.

LOVE LETTERS

I.

His elbow jerked in and out with the thick, massive, inky lines of his pen marks. My lines were thin and curvy; my *O*s fell on each other like a stack of deflated tires and my *L*s looked like yawning *C*s. But his letters looked like the clean, hard little houses you would expect of a boy. His *A* was a treehouse, his *H* a skyscraper. And his *T* was part Cross and part telephone pole. It rose up off the page as if it was 3-D, while mine barely peaked above the other letters and fell forward like a limp flag.

He looked exactly the way I should've looked. All sharp corners and neat edges, he had solid, dark eyes, and, unlike the rest of us in that Catholic school, he fit his skin. He was a boy and knew it. What's more, he knew exactly what a boy should be doing. How much trouble he should be getting into, how much rope he was allowed. I had no such clue, so I stayed clear of trouble and slunk in my chair behind his biggest-in-the-class back. When he shifted his arm or his head, I shifted mine, but as hard as I tried, I never matched him. His skin remained as perfect and unbroken as his ink.

II.

The architect of letters was splayed out on the trampoline in the backyard with a Coke bottle and a bag of Sugar Babies. He was shirtless, his hair was wet, and he smiled my way, then shouted for me to jump up with him. As soon as I did, he leapt up and down until the taut canvas bounced me off onto the grass and we both exploded in laughter.

"Fag," he wheezed out between laughs, then spat out a mouthful of Coke and threw the bag of candy my way. "Here you go, Fag."

I stood still for a moment as the air rushed in and out of my chest. Then I threw the bag back at him, jumped on the trampoline, and jumped into the air with that word ringing in my ear. "Fag." It wasn't a word I had heard before, but I knew instantly what it meant. "Fag." Only three letters long, but the sound rattled around my head until I was forced to say it myself. "Fag," I screamed out while I bounced, then tripped over a coil and fell back onto the grass.

The architect stood over me, tugged back on his Coke bottle, then spat a brown waterfall over my face. "Hey, let's turn on the water hose," he said. "Let's play Slip 'n' Slide!"

III.

I kept my face to the pillow until I was sure that he had fallen asleep. Then I opened my eyes and turned toward him. While I lay buttoned-up in a pair of Charlie Brown pajamas, he slept with both his shirt and his pants off, and the sight of him in

24

his underwear thrilled me. My ears burned and my throat was dry and I knew it. I knew that it hadn't been a joke; I knew that I was what he had said. I was a fag. That's why the Sisters frowned on me at Immaculate Heart. That's why my letters were all curlicues, feathers and fans, ribbons of silky ink.

But in the architect's bed, I didn't care that I couldn't match him, that my own letters failed. I lay next to him with the rustle of night crickets and the beat of his heart in my ear. I flattened out my hand and slid it under the curve of his arm. There was a little heat in that spot, and when I felt the heat, I pulled my hand back to my own pillow and pressed my face against my fingers. Then I fell asleep with the scent of a boy in my nose and the sting of three letters scratched into my skin, a fresh tattoo on my arm.

LYSOL WORKS

In our White House in Lafayette
the First Lady, my mother,

memorized her mother-in-law's
White Glove Test. It stuck in her mind

like a commercial: Cloroxed baseboards,
Windexed windows, and Lysol for smells.

Her memory kicked in one night
when she came home early and saw me

and two black friends in front of the TV.
Mama saw a mess to clean: she cut on the light,

cut off the TV. My two friends cut out the door.
I wanted to break away too when she broke out

with the can of Lysol. "God it stinks," she declared.
But I heard only the commercial. Lysol works.

"NOT THAT KIND
OF ANGEL"

she said, "A Charlie's Angel—you know, like
Farrah Fawcett?"

And I saw it, saw my sister with feathered hair,
streaked from a bottle of Sun-In, a knit halter top
stretched tight as cellophane against her breasts. I
saw her racing down the halls at school with a
pistol in her hand. Jumping in the window of a
white Cobra, throwing the stick shift into gear.
Speeding through the gravel parking lot, taking
turn after turn as if her tires were greased for the
ride. She hung her head out the window, laughed
at all the other girls' breasts. Weren't they swollen
little pimple titties? Weren't they eraserhead tits?
Weren't her tits better? They'd win her dates with
the quarterback, the class president. All the kids
and teachers in the hallway, the auditorium,
wouldn't they stand back in amazement now, in
absolute awe, for these surely were A+ top-of-the-
class gold-star head-cheerleader most-popular-girl
at–Acadiana Junior High *breasts*.

"Mama better watch out," she said again. "I'm fixing to become an angel."

And then I saw what she really meant. She'd wait
until she dragged home another detention note,
another expulsion, another report card dripping
red ink. Wait until Mama burst into another fuming
fit, until the fire of Mama's hands lit into her, until

the belt buckle flamed over her head. Then she'd twist her torso around, cup her two atomic tits, and *glare*. She'd take that extra step, too, find the words she'd been missing. Even if there wasn't a molecule of truth in anything she was about to say, she'd say it anyway. She'd look dead straight at Mama, shoot her sassy mouth.

"You just can't keep your hands off me, can you, can you?"

When Mama's hands fell to her side, she'd flip her feathered hair back, snap her halter top

and let her wings drop.

LOUISIANA

has a sense of humor
when it comes to election time and governors,
but not a clue
as to how to hide its problems.

The mouth of the Delta, too big for secrets,
keeps dumping trash into the Gulf.
And everyone knows
how crooked the Mississippi is.

EULOGY II

Already there are stories
that will never be told again,

stories Mama will forbid:
she never totaled Dad's company car,

never smoked that hash;
we never found a bottle

of Southern Comfort at her feet.
"An accident," Mama will say

in the same clipped voice she used
whenever a neighbor asked

about the bruises on her daughter's arms,
or the red welts on her hands. "An accident,"

she'll say, clasping her hands like a saint's
mother. The cover-up has begun,

I can't see my sister's body, the coffin reveals
only her head, her hands. Soon the coffin

will be shut. Soon we'll throw dirt on her grave.
She's gone, my sister is gone.

I tried to kiss her just now,
soft on the forehead, but my lips froze

and I was sure she'd bruise or turn brown
like the skin of a magnolia bud.

Even her hair that Mama sprayed back
seems too brittle to touch,

and the rosary that snakes though her hands
makes her look like a corroding icon.

SOUTHERN HOMES

Mama shut me up
at the funeral home
where we laid out

my sister for viewing.
"We have guests," she said.
"Show some hospitality."

HER STORY

I.

Jealous. No, I'm not jealous. Why would I be jealous? Did you hear? Did you? Your sister called me jealous. Do I look like a jealous woman to you? Don't answer. I don't need you to answer. I don't need your accusations. Your sister's had me on trial ever since she came back to this house. Jealous. Yellow. Born yellow. My little jaundiced baby born jealous.

II.

I sure as hell didn't put that mark on her forehead. That brown strawberry birthmark on her forehead leading her around so it was the first thing people noticed. "Marked," people would mumble under their breath in the Piggly-Wiggly, the Piccadilly, at the park, "That girl is marked." You think I gave her the evil eye, don't you?

III.

You oughta know what kind of hell I've been through since she left. It wasn't right your sister going off like that. There are four placemats at this table. Four chairs. We order a bucket of chicken, there's no one to eat the wings. We're a three-legged table now. No kind of family. What did your sister want? Why did she wreck? So much time is past. Stop asking questions, stop bringing her back. She's a ghost in this room now. And that's no kind of family.

IV.

"Something sick in me." Well if that wasn't the stray pup calling the bitch rabid. I should've kept her on a leash 'til she had her shots. But she'd have gnawed through the rope or yelped to her father 'til he unleashed her. I never would've let her go. Never wanted her to go. I said No. You have to know I said No.

V.

You wanna see pictures of the wreck? I'll show you a wreck. Look at your father here. Weak in the knees. Knees like pudding on a plate 'cause he thought he saw his little saint walk in the door and sit down at the table. Now look at him glow. First time I've seen the man glow since she left. This is a man? A man would haul that girl out back, peel off a good strip from that fig tree, and make her suffer for all the worry she buried in my bones. A wreck is what you wanna see? Don't forget it was your sister behind the wheel, not me. Don't forget it was your father who let her leave, not me. He let her walk out the door. He let her leave with the Southern Comfort. The sass in her mouth, the sting of liquor on her tongue. She stole his company car. Stole whatever she could get her hands on. Stole her way right out of here. Leaving me with you two sorry excuses for men. One a sure as hell pansy, the other might as well be. Where's my way out? Where's my little saint?

VI.

It was the night, well you know what night it was. There we were, your father lying in bed and me kneeling over a rosary same as always when I got to trembling and the roar of a train struck my ear. And you know we don't live near the tracks. A train roar just like the sound that tornado made before it tore the roof off our old house. Good thing I was kneeling or I would've rolled off the bed in fright. "Sweet Jesus," I said out loud. Your father sat up in bed, but didn't say a word like he was deaf, dumb, and mute. But I could tell in his eyes he was seeing what I saw. A Great Light from under our door. I opened the door and jumped back. That light lit up the hallway bright as a thousand burning bulbs, bright as a whole room on fire. When I squinted, I could see The Great Light was coming from under her bedroom. Just as I saw that, the light vanished — Poof! — and it was pitch dark again. Only now tiny beads of water covered my face. Not sweat. I wasn't sweating. This was a mist. I looked at your father, he was covered, too. That was no ghost, son, that was your sister.

VII.

That sister of yours. Your father's little saint. Look

at her halo spinning like a frisbee on top her head. Look at her.

Look at this mess. Gimme a hand, will you? You're the only one ever helped me 'round here. A good son. You helped me keep this house clean. Hand me the bleach, will you, sugar?

HURRICANE NAMES

Jungle Bunny
Pickaninny
Jigaboo

Spade
Porch Monkey
Nigger

These are the names I remember,
names for black people
in the South.

As with hurricanes
from the Gulf,
I remember the names,

remember where
the winds twisted, where
the tails slapped down

in the furious storms
which spun from the center
to clean everything in their path.

Mama started in the center, too
then worked her sponge
in tight circles, cleaning the house

with unstoppable force
and a powerful liquid
she called Hurricane in a Bottle.

She put bleach in the clothes,
the dishes, the toilets,
on the tile floors and baseboards.

Her declaration, even to herself,
was always the same:
Can't get things white enough.

Don't come home with no nigger
or you got no home.
Mama doesn't remember saying it

but she must have,
it's all I heard the first time
I lay under a black man.

He raised a storm
darker than dirt,
darker than blood when it dries.

I couldn't get clean enough,
couldn't halt the roaring in my ears
the hurricane of names.

SUNSPOTS

A good linebacker needs a good excuse:
too close to the sun, my juicy mouth

soaking you in, good as a woman's,
I had you burning up, I had you confused.

Yes, a good linebacker needs a good joke,
so you'll laugh and ask the team,

"How can you tell a woman's mouth
from a man's?" Then boast about how you had me

on my knees in a flash. Praise
my tight white ass that blinded you

like sunspots. I bet you'll forget
to say how tender my nipples were,

how firm and smooth my vanilla-wafer chest,
or how I shut up when you split

me, wiped yourself clean, left me,
under the bleachers, far from the sun.

DIRECTIONS

A linebacker
back at Carencro High explained:
I could kiss him anywhere,
he said,
except his mouth.

GRAPEPRINTS

You slap the last handful
of raisins in my mouth,

dried, shriveled, drained
of juice. Only the meat remains.

No wine left in a raisin's vein.
No fruit even, no sticky kiss.

Nothing but grapeprints
to mark my fingertips,

stain the skin brown.
No body should taste so odd, so good.

FALLOUT

I can't explain how molecules
join to make water.

I never grasped how two sticks
rubbing together make fire.

But when fire and water fuse,
I know what comes of it.

You
are simple to me.

HIS STORY

Birthright is not a confection, though sweet
to grow up with June Cleaver,

Father Knows Best, reruns
of Ricky Nelson. It's not sweet

watching friends fail to match Mike Brady, fail
even to pay rent by the first.

Before the age of twenty-five,
I was subpoenaed for the crime

of underachievement. "What's the deal
with your generation?" Dad asked.

"I went so much farther than my father —
It was my birthright, your birthright."

Birthright is still Dad's favorite gun
when he approaches the topic

of my failure to commit to just one
person, place, or job. But he talks

with more caution now, no longer placing
the basket of blame at his son's feet.

"You were robbed," he says, "of the sweet life
you deserve." He's seen articles,

43

he knows what's up. "Those immigrants,
those boat people coming here

breeding like niggers," he says. "They sit down
in a diner, smiling, nodding

while munching on a jelly donut
served by my first and only

son, my boy, the one I gave my name to."
That way, Dad rewrites history:

his son is not lazy, not criminal, no sir,
his son is a victim.

COFFEE BREAK

Last week, my parents bought me a coffee mug
emblazoned with a laser printout of my dead sister.

Last month, she appeared in their bedroom door
wrapped in a fuzzy ball of light. When she was six

and eight, and thirteen, she appeared in our backyard
wrapped in long cotton sleeves to hide the bruises.

But now she shines, up there next to the Pope,
rules the coffee shelf, my Saint Commodity.

THE TRIP

From his palm,
I take a hit

whose fingers slip
behind my eyes to pull down the shades.

His fingers shift
in my ass. I'm white hot.

All I remember
of what my friend said:

Mardi Gras's not a party, it's a trip.

NO STORY

We undressed each other, craving
only fodder for our stories.

A competition to award the best writer
the best lover, when neither

of us was either. We undressed
and watched each other,

but we were both afraid
and our tongues moved like dough.

With no heat between us,
no story, we just froze.

YOU CAN'T ALWAYS GET
WHAT YOU WANT

is what you said, a line you picked up
from the Stones, the same song
booming now

from speakers behind the bar.
I laughed,
thinking you meant to be funny.

Drunk on the sounds,
dizzy from the beer,
I barely heard what you said next:

It was a little thing we had.

I admired the way each word fell
from your lips,
like snow falling on snow,

but little things like snow
stop people from leaving home,
keep them from getting what they need.

REVOLVER

Leave it to my uncle to clear up the whole
mess. AIDS is not a plague, but a blessing

from God. It's the homo himself who's
the pariah, the problem.

A mortal sin, he calls it, same as murder.
AIDS is not a plague, but a revolver.

Son, he says, you're shooting fair game.
You're shooting yourself.

HOW DO YOU SPELL

rape when you're on a date?
How do you say no when you

first said yes? How do you say stop
when you're the one who started?

Men don't say stop, say no.
Men don't rape each other.

Don't pull out the stops, he said.
Don't cuff my hands. It was you

kissing me like a bandit, you making out
like a thief. Then he threw me

over and around,
like he was looking for something.

KEN DOLL

I wanted to fuck David Duke
Grand Marshall of the KKK

Ken Doll candidate for Governor.
I wanted to fuck David Duke

so I did.
He was tight, but he couldn't resist,

he needed all the votes he could get.
His face barely moved. Still, I knew

he wanted more. When I woke
my roommate said, "Duke's

been elected governor." Under the covers
I checked my drawers, felt the dry

white sheets but said nothing. I knew
that was Louisiana's dream, not mine.

SHE SHOT HIM DOWN

Maybe I shouldn't read celebrity bios
or maybe I shouldn't listen
to people talk on the #7 train downtown,

but it was all I could do to keep from screaming,
"Fuck Frank Sinatra!"
when these two were going on

about how they wanted to party
with Frank, Mr. Croon,
The Voice, Ol' Blue Eyes himself.

"She shot me down," he sang.

I wish she had, Frank,
I wish she had shot you down
before you shed your liberal skin

like the fork-tongued lizard you were,
before the lizard became a rat,
before the rat formed The Rat Pack.

I wish she had shot you down
before I heard you say
all you know about singing

you learned from Billie Holiday.
What did you learn about being black?
About lynch mobs?

Or maybe that's what you were doing
in Sun City: research.
Frank, Frank, you gray grizzly,

it's hibernation time,
time for bears like you
to feed on their own fat.

I come to bury, not to praise.
I come to watch worms
swim like spaghetti in your saucy remains.

Go to sleep, Frank.
I'll do a dance on your marble grave
and curse your Catholic name.

MISSING

Have you seen me lately? I'm not
the 9 ½–year-old kid who disappeared

only to reappear on your milk carton,
last seen wearing khaki shorts.

I come up short in the papers.
Though I'm older than milk

and the Missing Persons Bureau,
there are few pictures of me.

I'm not homogenized,
but homosexual,

just an issue,
a rash, a disease,

a troublesome thing,
last seen wearing nothing.

BURGUNDY

My arms stretch across more than a decade
by the time you return from the army
with an ache to touch something familiar.

Perhaps I'll love you for returning
to touch blue gray moss
which hangs from tree limbs

like old lady's hair—it only seems dead.
Perhaps I'll love you for returning
to touch mimosa blossoms,

pine needles, fat figs shaped
like testicles and tears. Perhaps.
But when your tongue returns

to touch my Southern heart,
to empty its chambers, you'll choke
and I'll cough and the half glass of me

will still be too much for you.
We'll both turn the color of burgundy
and say it's good to be together again.

HYMN

I search for you between the shoulders
of each pew I pass, pray for your return inside

the lines of "Evil" and "Amen." When the priest's
arms spread, he offers salvation, a hymn, but not
you.

I KNOW SOMEDAY

maybe ten years down the water
when they get bored with all

else they own, they'll turn to us:
Aren't they unusual?

Aren't they rare?
Someday we'll all be set

under glass, magnified
a thousand times over

but even with the eye
of God, they won't know

what to do with us.
So they'll sell us

and the buyers will say,
So strange! So queer!

Only ten percent! We'll
fetch a good price

then they'll sell us
back to ourselves.

S H H H

We don't want anyone
to hear American Lit's

Best Kept Secret. All of its best
writers are not white

not straight, not male.
All of its best writers

don't lie. They crack
secrets open like eggs.

Shhh. If you listen
you can hear them fry.

CIRCE

She turned men into
swine, water into

water. She made men
whine whine whine

and squeal like pigs.
She had taste and a sense

of humor you could see
bunch up like a muscle

as she lifted the men
into air, into tender flight.

NO PLACE

I don't know why I keep walking. By the time
I reach you, my feet will blister and crack.

I'll give up the futon, Wild Turkey on the rocks,
tuxedo shirts, meat, leather, sucking cocks,

The Price Is Right, bleached hair, peanut butter, *Playgirl,*
jazz, jasmine, jacking-off, *The Wizard of Oz,*

James Joyce, James Dean, Jim Morrison, Jesus Christ.
When I reach you, my clothes will peel

like dried flesh. My spirit will pucker and break.
Then I'll stop walking, stop dropping things and say:

"The year isn't light, the road isn't yellow."
And I'll be where you are, and I'll be no place.

THE BAYOU LOUNGE

in Baton Rouge is where you'll come back
to suck my fingers, search my ears

with your tongue for the breaths you put there
during that sticky summer when

even the live oaks were sweating. Rain
was untying the ribbons of moss

on the bending bayou where we sat
watching an old man's fingers

trace the hull of his pirogue for trouble.
That was when you laid the trouble

on me, said there were holes in my toes
so that long ago I had slipped out

of my body like silt from the bank
into the bayou. You tried swimming after

me, but I blended with the muddy foam.
Twisting currents and a dozen

angry whirlpools worked against you.
By then, so tired and out of breath

you stopped trying. But I didn't stop,
won't stop now. I tell my story

to anyone who listens. Each time
they burst out laughing at the end

where you say, "Like the weather
in Louisiana, you bring me down."

In the Bayou State, we learn to forgive
the weather. But at The Bayou Lounge

we skip the forgiveness, we just
order another round.

LIVE OAK

In Louisiana, on a farm past the farthest bayou, but this side the warm waters of the Gulf, there lived a boy named Tee. Whatever Tee knew, he learned from his marble-eyed grampa. Paw-Paw taught him to kiss dogs and read poetry, to walk barefoot on shell and gravel, to speak Cajun and chop okra, to hop around like a rain frog, calling down the rain. He taught him to sit on the floor, to be suspicious of furniture and strangers. But, more than anything else, Paw-Paw taught him to stay away from other boys. Getting close to one, he said, could only get Tee into trouble.

Tee often sat alone under the oldest live oak on the farm, and he liked to imagine the tree's history, to pretend it had known his ancestors. That tree was older than old, his grampa told him, older than sleep. "Ça c'est vieux," he said, snatching a piece of moss from one of its branches. But when it came to the live oak, Tee knew more than his grampa. It was, after all, his tree, the only place he could go when he needed to feel like himself.

Early one November, near nightfall, Tee sat snugly between the largest of the tree's exposed roots, running his fingers in the deep grooves of the bark, when all of a sudden a breeze began to twitch and turn in the limbs of the tree. It moved off the branches, releasing some leaves. It searched for a shape, gathering dust, twigs, pebbles as it went. The breeze grew stronger, circling, hugging, squeezing the tree. Purplish-red leaves slipped down the trunk. The trunk itself shook, as if it might explode.

Then, faster than Tee's eyes could follow, the branches of the oak twisted into muscle and flesh, twisted into fingers. One hand glided along the bark of the trunk flattening it into a smooth, bare chest. Roots melted into legs. Burnt-gold leaves twirled into soft curls. And the treetop softened into a boy's fresh fiery face.

Tee was transfixed; he couldn't move. He thought the tree-boy too beautiful to watch. He thought this was something coming out of him. Tee even thought for a moment that he was looking at himself. But when he reached out his hand to touch the boy, he heard his grampa shout, "Stop!" hopping up and down on the porch, flailing his arms. "Don't, don't," he shouted, "don't touch that boy. We don't know him." But Tee couldn't help it; he had no choice. He reached out his hand, cupped the boy's chin, kissed him lightly on the lips.

Tee took a step back toward his grampa. But it was too late; a charge ran through him. Looking down, he saw that his hands were glowing. Then he saw that his arms were glowing too. His legs, feet, all he could see of himself was glowing, brighter and brighter until he threatened to upset the sky, to turn night into day. Brighter and brighter until he burst.

BLOW CHARMS

I've made you come,
and you've made me cry
for the last time.

You pound and pound
at me unwrapped,
but won't let me play roles,

suck your nipples:
"No milk in them."
You never sucked me off,

probably a bottle baby
spoon-fed too soon.
You talk about hot-buttered dick

with Häagen-Dazs vanilla,
but you won't eat what I have
and you won't bag it,

claiming you can't feel
that way. Well, feel this,
Mister, I'm done starving.

These Butterfingers won't melt in your hands,
those Hershey's Kisses won't come in my mouth,
I've had enough Blow Charms.

MOVIE STAR

I wanted to fuck Ronald Reagan
MGM Matinee Idol, GE Merchant

Movie Star Candidate for President.
I wanted to fuck Ronald Reagan

so I did.
He performed like a star.

Emoting on cue,
he collected votes like ticket stubs.

His hair never moved. Still, I knew
he would hit his mark. When I woke

my grandfather said, "Reagan's
been elected President." I felt the cold

plastic slip on the bed. I knew
that was his dream, not mine.

VENICE BEACH VENUS

This queen is different. She walks in languor,
not arriving anywhere,
yet talks so fast, laughs so hard,
tickles you into going along.

Red hair says she's no one's Venus,
no one's clay, no one's canvas.

But her pockets are spent; giving's her liquor.
She wants to touch you, kiss you there.
Ask what has her sick, thin, tired,
she throws back her head, explodes into song.

Call her no one's Venus,
she won't say you're wrong.

IMMACULATE HEART

Drop your blade on an emblazoned scar. Let it close like a bent orchid, a bleeding jewel.

THE BATTLE OF
OUR UNION

The twitch of your lips,
the tap of my razor,
the battle of our union

reduced to maneuvers:
the charge of your body,
the retreat of my hand,

your fist, my nose,
blood on my T-shirt,
the jackknife tattoo on your arm,

the clump of my words, the punch of yours.
The twitch of your lips,
the tap of my razor, the battle.

REFRAIN

If you were born a little later, I could call you
Boy. You know if I could nurture, I'd mother you.

If you were born a little sooner, I could call you
Daddy. You know if I could murder, I'd smother you.

MOJO

see my fingers rise like smoke
see them fall like ash

you're mine now, song
prayer and plea

whatever you heard is wrong
I'll never set you free

feel my breath
hear my whisper

together we'll rise and fall
rise and fall

FATHER, THE WAR

that you told me stories
of was sexy. As you boasted

about battles and thunder,
I got a thrill. A picture

shot in my head of me pinned
to the mat, a fluttering

silver moth, making love
to a soldier while he was

making war, wings crushed
like cities. Father, the war caught

fire, burned off in just six weeks
like some brief, mad

affair in someone else's bed.
My eyes blazed, a trembling

black tiger in jail, fur burned
like fields. Father, the war wasn't

sexy even with men all around me,
protesters, priests and soldiers

a clash of men trying to clutch
each other, leaving marks

hickies, small bites, light bruises
like sacred but errant purple hearts.

SOLDIER OF THE PAST

Back from the army, you fall
at my feet, the ones you kissed

once with a burgundy tongue.
"Back in my arms," you say.

"Back on the same road, too."
And you're right:

it is the same road,
same gravel-pocked bayou road

where you left me
where you've come back,

ten years late in a pickup
black with stickers and decals.

The same road where twice
you slammed into deer

one buck, one doe,
then turned to me with crimson eyes.

You pin me down, rifle under my chin,
rifle between my legs.

"I've missed this," you say,
still talking between quotes,

ramming yourself into me still,
taking aimless shots.

You'll never reach me; I know that now.
The road ends soon

and there's a bus. Hear your dog tags
jingle, that old song?

NO COLOR

That crimson tattoo on your thigh,
you can't forget him. He rubs

between your legs when you run,
hot coals to your skin and all sighs.

His lips are bigger than Brando's,
his sweat sweeter than your own.

Blue-black and yellow-brown,
he chases color trails down

his chest. Ropy arms and dark eyes,
he fucks you into rhythm until you are

drunk, jumbled, mixed up, spying
every shade, but making out no color.

DISCOVERY

this discovery they made that we have no need
for the womb; the human fetus can live in a jar

this discovery you made that you have no need
for me; the single gay man can live in a bar

one more discovery and soon we'll be born
without a navel, a clue, a scar

CLASS CLOWN

I wanted to fuck George W. Bush
Class Clown, Boy Cheerleader

Coked-up Candidate for Prez.
I wanted to fuck George W. Bush

so I did.
He fell to his knees

like a born-again pledge.
Like a man in need of a vote

his eyes never moved. Still, I knew
he wanted what I had. When I woke

my father said, "W.'s
been elected president." I pulled

my dirty drawers down. I knew
that was America's dream, not mine.

DECALOGUE
('85 - '95)

I.

The test had been handled by a plasma donor center, where I went under the needle twice a week in exchange for extra cash for all the booze and tabs of acid that fueled my early college days. One day I walked in for my usual "donation," but the nurse gave me the fish-eye then looked at my folder with alarm, and I thought, *Good Lord, they found out I'm diabetic.* I thought, *Holy shit, they found LSD in my blood.* I thought, *Sweet Jesus, they found out I'm gay*— maybe the black tights, tuxedo jacket, and twenty-four-inch pearls gave me away.

II.

Besides, I *was* gay, wasn't I? So the test results were no surprise. All kinds of terrible afflictions had been promised me. I was *supposed* to catch AIDS; it was part of the plan, the price I had to pay. My father had said that AIDS was God's revenge, that my being gay was like shooting myself in the foot, that homosexuality was the same as murder or suicide in the eyes of the Lord. Hadn't Mama warned me about eyes going blind and body parts falling off?

III.

While waiting for the second blood test, I OD'd at a three-keg pool party. My girlfriend had tired of my perpetual mid-party pass-outs, so she ordered me to do a handful of speed. I did two, then two more. Within an hour, I fell into a fit of convulsions, my eyes froze open, the pool party cleared, and two ambulances and a fire truck followed the final two rounds of speed. I was surrounded by men in uniform when I heard her say, "I have no idea what happened. We were just sitting here talking when he fell on the floor and started choking on his tongue." She said it so casually; it was like she was describing a glass shaken off the counter by a mysterious vibration.

IV.

My parents each made the sign of the Cross when the therapist announced there was nothing wrong with me, nothing a few cures wouldn't fix. I wasn't gay, not really. It was an illusion or delusion, like the false positive of the HIV test. All I had to do was to stop wearing black eyeliner and rosary beads, to give up the tube skirts and tuxedo jackets. I had to read the sports pages and memorize game scores. Stop dying my hair magenta and listening to the Sisters of Mercy. "Change your behavior," he said, "and you change."

V.

When I reached San Francisco, I found the wild-eyed riot I had been looking for. First ACT UP, then Queer Nation and an explosion of gay clubs in the SOMA warehouse district. Ecstasy and house music crashed down on the city like a white tidal wave. In the Gold Room at Colossus, a sea of hands rose to the ceiling over a crest of white crew-neck T-shirts. In the main room, a twenty-foot-high stack of speakers pumped out the crackling anthem of the moment. "Everybody's free," the song said. Then another threw down the challenge, "Are you ready to fly?"

VI.

I was fumbling through words, trying to describe how long it had been, how little I'd tried, when he put a finger to my lips and said that all my talk was turning him on. He wanted to take me home and show me everything. How to stroke and bite his nipple, how to lick the curve of his underarm. How to press the spot between his legs to delay an orgasm. How to put on a condom without losing the heat of the moment. How to enter him from behind, from the side, from on top. How to spread my own legs and rock under him. How to find a rhythm and how to hold it with a really long kiss. How to keep my eyes open and let my skin catch fire.

VII.

He had gotten high on smack and swallowed some guy's cum in the back of a bar. Instead of nodding sympathetically, I burst into a near-rage, "How could you?" I demanded. "How could you forget about everything you taught me?"

But when I saw his eyes sink back in his head, I forgot my fury and kissed him on the lips. "It's all right," I said. "Just be careful, baby. Be careful." I really meant "Be safe." Less than six months later, he tested positive for HIV and my heart sank. I had been too hard on him. I hadn't said the right thing. I hadn't saved him.

VIII.

A charge ran through my body as I thought, *this is it, this is what all the excitement was about, this is what it feels like to fuck a guy without a condom.* My legs and his legs locked together and my eyes shut down on a dream: I was in a tent near a bayou in Louisiana and I could hear water running nearby. I was safe, safe in a tent with a boy squirming under me. I put my lips to his mouth and let my tongue find its way inside. I rocked and thrust and eased my way in and out of him until he finally flipped me over and slipped inside. Afterwards, I felt nothing, only exhaustion and the curly edges of sleep.

IX.

A friend and I sat in an East Village bar as I told him what had happened. After I got through stammering and fidgeting, he let his sharp, but quiet gaze fall down on me. Eye to eye, we stayed still and silent until he raised his hand from the table and brought it hard and fast against my face. "What the fuck were you thinking?" he said. "Have you forgotten everything?"

X.

And I realized that I had. I had forgotten the scare of the false positive test, the feeling that I was going to die. I had forgotten the marches and the banners and the sight of my roommate covered in lesions. I had forgotten my friends who had already died, Bill and Kelly and Charlie and Jeff and Malcolm and Francis and Daniel and Chris and Roger and Clinton.

Ten years passed, a decade, and I've changed that little. Or maybe I've changed so much that I've come full circle. I'll have to get tested again, and again I'll have to wait for the results. I'll sit tracing my hands over my body looking for trouble spots. Listening for a hollow murmur, a dull echo. Staring in the mirror waiting to go blind. Plucking out an eye, a black pearl.

SOUTH

is not a place;
it's a direction.